THE SESAME STREET LIBRARY

With Jim Henson's Muppets

VOLUME 7

FEATURING
THE LETTERS
N, O AND P
AND THE NUMBER
7

Children's Television Workshop/Funk & Wagnalls, Inc.

WRITTEN BY:

Michael Frith
Emily Perl Kingsley
David Korr
Sharon Lerner
Nina B. Link
Jeffrey Moss
Norman Stiles
Daniel Wilcox

ILLUSTRATED BY:

A. Delaney
Michael Frith
Joseph Mathieu
Marc Nadel
Michael J. Smollin
Bob Taylor
Kay Wood

PHOTOGRAPHS BY:

Charles P. Rowan

A Rain Poem

I love the rain because the flowers
All need the rain to help them grow.
I sit inside and watch for hours,
And I don't mind because I know
The daffodils outside the windowpane
Agree with me—and really love the rain.

What a dumb reason to love the rain!

I love it when it pours down without stopping
'Cause everyone gets *soaked* from head to toe.
Their hair gets wet, their shoes
 and socks are sopping,
They step in puddles everywhere they go.

Listen to those people all complain (heh, heh)—
And *that* is why us Grouches love the rain.

Look out! Here comes a taxi!
Oh! That was beautiful!

I love the rain...and when the raindrops
Fall so softly from the sky,
I go outside with my umbrella
And COUNT THEM as they're
dropping by.
And the reason that I really love them
Is because there are so many of them.
Ha, ha, ha!

WONDERFUL!
WONDERFUL!

We all love the rain for different reasons—
It doesn't matter that we don't agree,
For something that is wonderful to you, friend,
May be something else entirely to me.

So if I love the rain because of flowers...

And soggy things and mud
just make me sing...

And I could count the drops
that fall for hours...

We all agree at least on one small thing—
We love the rain!

Hello.

I, Grover, am going to tell you some poems all about three friends of mine. And their names all begin with the letter **O**.

I like Ogden Ox . . . he really is neat.

Except when he's dancing and steps on my feet.

Olive the Octopus
has many charms.

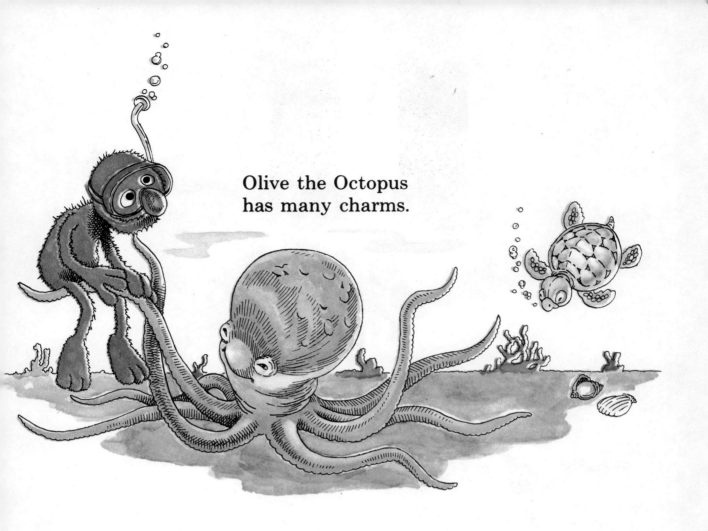

Except when she hugs me
with all of her arms.

OH
OH!

Ollie the Ostrich
is very well bred.

Except when he's tired
and sits on my head.

Well, those are all the **O** poems
I have time for today. I do not
think I am going to do any more
for a long, long time. Good-by.
O o o o o o o o o o o o o h.

Big Bird's Shape Story

Goldie-Snuffle and the Seven Bears

One day a beautiful, golden-haired Snuffle-upagus named Goldie-Snuffle was walking through the woods with her friend Big Bird.

"Goldie," said Big Bird, "you have never met *any* of my friends, and they all say there is no such thing as a Snuffle-upagus. Will you come meet my friends, **the 7 Bears**? They live right around the corner."

"Oh, goody!" said Goldie-Snuffle.

Big Bird and Goldie-Snuffle came to the cottage of the **7** Bears. They knocked on the door, but nobody answered. "There's nobody home, Goldie," said Big Bird.

"Oh, dear," said Goldie-Snuffle. "Well let's go in anyway." And in they went.

Inside the cottage were **7** chairs. "I think I'll sit down," said Goldie-Snuffle.

Big Bird said, "But, Goldie, some of these chairs are small, some are big, and some are in-between. How do you know which chair is just right for you?"

"I'll sit in them all," said Goldie-Snuffle.

So she sat in all of the chairs, one at a time. And she broke all of the chairs… one at a time.

"They were *all* too small for you, Goldie," said Big Bird.

Next, Goldie-Snuffle found a
table with **7** bowls of spaghetti
on it.

Goldie-Snuffle said, "Some of
these bowls of spaghetti
are too hot, and some of them are
too cold, and some are just
right. But I really love
spaghetti, so I think
I'll eat them all."

And she did.

When she finished eating, Goldie-Snuffle said, "I think I'll lie down."

In the cottage were **7** beds.

Big Bird said, "Goldie, some of these beds are small, some are big, and some are in-between. But they're all too small for you."

"Then I'll lie down on them all at once," said Goldie-Snuffle.

And she did. And she broke them all at once.

"Oh, dear," said Goldie-Snuffle, "I have to go. So long, Bird."

"But Goldie," said Big Bird, "the cottage is a mess, and the **7** Bears are just getting home. Stay and help clean up."

"I'd like to, Bird, but it's time for my nap," said Goldie-Snuffle. And she left.

When the **7** Bears saw their house, they said, "My goodness! Somebody broke all our chairs…"

"…and ate all our spaghetti…"

"…and crushed all our beds. Big Bird, what happened?"

"Oh, I can explain," said Big Bird. "Goldie-Snuffle was here. She's a beautiful, golden-haired Snuffle-upagus, and she loves spaghetti, and she's very big, and..."

"*Snuffle-upagus?*" said the **7** Bears. "There's no such thing as a Snuffle-upagus. Big Bird, you sure have some imagination!"

Cookie Monster's Surprise Cookies

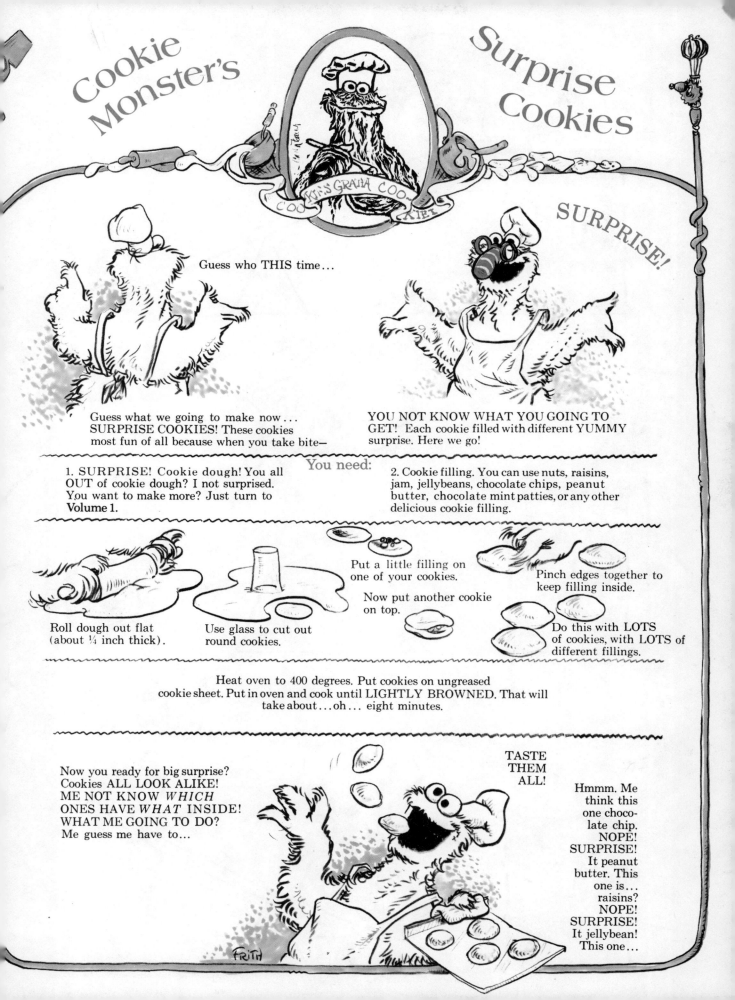

SURPRISE!

Guess who THIS time...

Guess what we going to make now... SURPRISE COOKIES! These cookies most fun of all because when you take bite—

YOU NOT KNOW WHAT YOU GOING TO GET! Each cookie filled with different YUMMY surprise. Here we go!

You need:

1. SURPRISE! Cookie dough! You all OUT of cookie dough? I not surprised. You want to make more? Just turn to **Volume 1.**

2. Cookie filling. You can use nuts, raisins, jam, jellybeans, chocolate chips, peanut butter, chocolate mint patties, or any other delicious cookie filling.

Roll dough out flat (about ¼ inch thick).

Use glass to cut out round cookies.

Put a little filling on one of your cookies.

Now put another cookie on top.

Pinch edges together to keep filling inside.

Do this with LOTS of cookies, with LOTS of different fillings.

Heat oven to 400 degrees. Put cookies on ungreased cookie sheet. Put in oven and cook until LIGHTLY BROWNED. That will take about...oh... eight minutes.

Now you ready for big surprise? Cookies ALL LOOK ALIKE! ME NOT KNOW *WHICH* ONES HAVE *WHAT* INSIDE! WHAT ME GOING TO DO? Me guess me have to...

TASTE THEM ALL!

Hmmm. Me think this one chocolate chip. NOPE! SURPRISE! It peanut butter. This one is... raisins? NOPE! SURPRISE! It jellybean! This one...

Snow White

One day Snow White's wicked stepmother, the queen, went to her magic mirror and asked: "Mirror, mirror on the wall. Who is the fairest one of all?"

The mirror answered, "Queen, you are full fair, 'tis true. But Snow White is fairer still than you."

The queen was so jealous that she told her footman to take Snow White into the woods and leave her there.

Snow White wandered in the woods until she came to a tiny house where seven little dwarfs lived. They were very happy to have the beautiful princess live with them.

But when the stepmother spoke to her mirror again, she discovered that Snow White was still alive. So she dressed up like an old hag and went to the tiny house in the woods. She gave Snow White a bite of a poisoned apple and the poor princess dropped dead—or so it seemed.

The sad dwarfs put the dead princess into a glass case so her beauty would be with them always. The next day a handsome prince rode by. Snow White looked so beautiful that he asked to take her to his castle. The sad little dwarfs agreed but, while they were hitching the glass case to a horse, they dropped it. The piece of apple fell out of Snow White's throat. She sat up and opened her eyes!

The happy prince took Snow White back to his castle, where they were married. The wicked queen never bothered the princess again.

Once upon a time, a nasty pirate sailed into a town. "Ahoy, mateys," the pirate announced. "My name is Pete the Pirate, and I am so nasty that I am going to take away everything in your town that begins with the letter **P**."

And immediately, he grabbed a bag of **peanuts** from the hand of a little girl and dropped it into his pirate sack.

"Heh, heh," chuckled Pete the Pirate, and before he had finished chuckling, he had grabbed a **pizza pie** from the hands of a pizza-maker and had thrown it into his pirate sack.

"There's only one thing you can do to stop me from taking all the **P** things in your town," said Pete the Pirate. "And that's to say a special word that begins with the letter **P**. If anyone says the special **P** word, then I'll stop and go away."

And with that, he picked up a little boy's **puppy** and threw it into his pirate sack.

The people of the town got together and tried to think of what the special **P** word might be. The mayor had an idea. So he marched right up to Pete the Pirate and announced, "**Pickle**!"

"**Pickle**?" said Pete the Pirate. "You think that's the word that will make me stop? Ha!"

And he grabbed the mayor's **pants** right off him and threw them into his pirate sack.

Then, just for good measure, he grabbed the **packages** from the arms of a passing lady, and a stray **pig** that was walking down the street. He threw them in his pirate sack, too.

The people of the town got together again to try to think of the special **P** word that would make the pirate stop taking things. The cook from the biggest restaurant in town had an idea. So when the pirate came into his kitchen, the cook yelled, "**Porcupine**!"

"**Porcupine**?" said the pirate. "You think that's the special word that will make me stop? You're a pretty silly cook, you know that?"

And with that, the pirate grabbed all the cook's **pots** and **pans** and threw them into his pirate sack. Then, just for good measure, he went through the town collecting all the **pillows** and **pianos** and threw them into his pirate sack, too.

Well, the people of the town were getting pretty upset when a little boy came up to the pirate just as he was pulling a **pair** of **pajamas** off the washline.

"Mr. Pirate," said the little boy, "won't you stop taking all the **P** things from our town?"

"Why should I?" said the pirate. "I'm nasty."

"*Please,*" said the littie boy.

"What did you say?" said the pirate.

"I said *please,*" said the little boy.

"That's it!" exclaimed the pirate. "That's the special word. **Please** is the special **P** word! I don't like you at all, little boy, but I'll have to stop because you said **please**."

And as quickly as Pete the Pirate had come to town, he left—and he never came back again.

The townspeople were grateful to the little boy. They only wished they had thought of the special **P** word sooner. Still, with the pirate gone, things could return to normal, and the people of the town all lived pretty happily ever after.

PEOPLE
IN YOUR
NEIGHBORHOOD
(Brought to you by Bert)

Bert's Box Town Neighborhood

Boy, am I proud of this . . . I made a box town for my friends, the Twiddlebugs. I've been collecting these nifty boxes for a long time. I guess you could find boxes of every shape in the whole world in my box town. If you want to collect boxes, then you can make a Twiddlebug box town, too.

What you'll need:

Boxes of all different shapes. Cereal boxes, oatmeal boxes, shoe boxes, milk and juice cartons, spaghetti boxes, etc.

Crayons, or paint

Glue

Some pieces of paper

Scissors

What you do:

1. With paper, and crayons or paint, decorate boxes to look like houses and stores.

2. Cut doors that open and close in the houses and stores.

3. You can even glue boxes one on top of another to make some apartment houses.

4. Trace the signs and Twiddlebug pictures below and paste them on the boxes.

5. You can use toy cars in your town, too.

POLICE STATION

Bakery

Fire Station

GROCER

DOCTOR BUG M.D. Specialist WINGS & FEELERS

J. Mathieu

Sam the Shoemaker

One day Maria was walking down the street
when she met Sam the Robot. "Where are you going?"
Sam asked. "To the shoemaker," Maria answered.
"The heel came off my shoe and I have to wear it tonight.
And I need to have my shoes shined, too."
"I will fix your shoe," said Sam. "I am a machine. I am perfect. I can do anything."
Maria thought for a minute. She had always taken her shoes to the shoemaker to be fixed. But she
didn't want to hurt Sam's feelings, so she dropped her shoe into Sam's hatch.

Bells rang! Lights flashed! And from deep
inside Sam came strange whirring and
hammering noises.
"Your shoe is now fixed," Sam said, and his
hatch popped open.
Maria pulled out her shoe. She looked at it.
"Sam," she said, "I'm afraid you made a
mistake. You put the heel on the front of the
shoe instead of on the back. Maybe I'll just
go to the shoemaker and he'll..."

"Wait!" said Sam. "I will fix your shoe. I am perfect. I will put the heel in the right place!"
Maria dropped the shoe back in and the lights started flashing again.

But this time when Sam was finished, he had put the heel in the *middle* of the shoe. "Sam," Maria tried to explain as she held up her other shoe (the one with the heel in the right place), "Sam, don't you see? These two shoes have to be *exactly* the same."

"I can do anything," said Sam. "Give me the two shoes." Maria put the two shoes in the hatch and waited. And this time, when the hatch opened, both shoes *were* exactly the same . . .

They *both* had heels in the middle.
"Sam," cried Maria, "what have you done to my shoes?"
"I have made them both the same," Sam explained. "Maria, where are you going? I have not shined your shoes yet."
"To the shoemaker!" Maria yelled as she ran down the street. "Now I've got to have *both* my shoes fixed."